A Parents Magazine
Read Aloud Original

TESS
AND
TIM

written by Marc Gave
drawings by Abby Carter

PARENTS MAGAZINE PRESS
NEW YORK

For Peter and Emma—M.G.
To P.J. and Buck—A.C.

Library of Congress Cataloging-in-Publication Data

Gave, Marc.
Tess and Tim.

Summary: An older brother describes what it is like
to live with his younger sister, Tess the pest.
[1. Brothers and sisters—Fiction.]   I. Carter,
Abby, ill.   II. Title.
PZ7.G235Te   1988   [E]   88-12418
ISBN 0-8193-1185-5

TESS THE PEST

This is my sister.
Her name is Tess.
She is a pest.

I guess I love her.
But she makes me mad.
Like the day
we went to the beach.

I showed her how
to ride the waves.

But she got water
in her eyes.
She cried and made me
take her out.

I gave her a sandwich
for lunch.
She had to open it up.

What a dumb thing to do.
I guess that's why
it's called a *sand*wich.

Later, I built a sand castle.
Tess wanted to help.

But she fell—SPLAT!—
and crushed it.

Not only is Tess a pest,
but so are her friends.
One day Joey came over.
He really liked my toy cars.

I chased them out of my room.
Mom took them to the kitchen.
She gave them paints.

Mom went to answer the door.
Tess and Joey painted
Puss the cat.

I had to hold Puss
while Mom gave her a bath.
That Tess sure is a pest!

MY BIRTHDAY DINNER

On my birthday, Mom and Dad
took me out to dinner.
Tess the pest came, too.

"Why does *she* have to come?"
I asked.
"Because she is your sister,"
Mom said.

We went to a fancy place.
There were cloth napkins
and real glasses.

Tess banged her glass
with her knife.
"You rang?" said the waiter.
I wanted to hide under the table.

Then Tess knocked over
the bread basket.

She tried to give me
a piece from the floor.

We had spaghetti to eat.
"Tess," said Mom,
"let me cut yours
in small pieces."

Before Mom had a chance,
Tess rolled her meatball
across the table.

Later, Tess blew bubbles
through her straw.

And she dropped
her ice cream.
She cried until the waiter
came with more.

But the worst thing was...
on the way home,
Tess gave me a kiss.

I wiped it off.
What a pest that Tess is!

MRS. WIGGLES, WHERE ARE YOU?

Last Friday, Grandma came.

Mom said, "Have fun
with Grandma while Dad
and I are away."

Grandma played with us
all afternoon.
Then *I* had to clean up.
She and Tess cooked supper.

We had tuna and noodles.
Tess and I liked the noodles.
Puss and Boots liked the tuna.

At bedtime, Grandma
told us a story.
I had heard it before.
But it was funny,
and I laughed.

Tess started to cry.
"Uh-oh," I said.
"Mrs. Wiggles is gone.
Tess never sleeps without her."

I looked in the kitchen.
I looked in the playroom.

I even looked in the washer.
Wasn't I a good brother?

Grandma hugged Tess.
But she just cried harder.
What a pest Tess was being.

I tried to remember the last
time I had seen Mrs. Wiggles.
Just then the phone rang.

It was Mom!

"How are you, sweetie?" she asked.

"Is something missing?"

"Mrs. Wiggles," I said.

"How did you know?"

Tess got on the phone.
Mom said, "Mrs. Wiggles
came to the hotel with us.
I know you miss her.
But she can't come home alone.
We'll bring her home soon."

Tess is a pest.
But she looked so sad.
I felt sorry for her.
I went and got Mr. Grizzly.

"Here," I said to Tess.
"You can sleep with *him*."
Tess looked at me.
She gave me a big kiss.

I didn't wipe it off.

About the Author

Before **Marc Gave** wrote children's books, he edited them. Although he still edits, he prefers writing, because he can use his own experience in his stories. He draws inspiration from his wife and two children, with whom he lives on Long Island, New York; from strange things that happen in the world daily; and from ideas that sometimes seem to come out of thin air.

About the Artist

Abby Carter is a freelance illustrator in New York City. She grew up in Maine with three brothers of her own. Her brothers never thought their young sister a pest—until she began to sell little drawings to gift shops for her pocket money. (*They* were stuck with mowing lawns.) She now lives with her husband, Doug, and her cat, Bosco, on Long Island, New York.